T0082541

Love We Make

JL Hansen

LOVE WE MAKE

iUniverse books may be ordered through booksellers or by contacting:

iUniverse
1663 Liberty Drive
Bloomington, IN 47403
www.iuniverse.com
844-349-9409

*Because of the dynamic nature of the Internet, any web addresses or
links contained in this book may have changed since publication and
may no longer be valid. The views expressed in this work are solely those
of the author and do not necessarily reflect the views of the publisher,
and the publisher hereby disclaims any responsibility for them.*

*Any people depicted in stock imagery provided by Getty Images are
models, and such images are being used for illustrative purposes only.
Certain stock imagery © Getty Images.*

ISBN: 978-1-6632-4933-3 (sc)
ISBN: 978-1-6632-4932-6 (e)

Library of Congress Control Number: 2022923657

Print information available on the last page.

iUniverse rev. date: 12/27/2022

Thank you Erin N Bacon of Destiny Studio's
and Craig Baker for the amazing photos.

I can't believe she dragged me out like this—literally dragged me by my oversized grandpa sweater. She didn't even let me comb my hair, so messy bun it is. I was lying on the couch with a bag of Cool Ranch Doritos, wearing my Captain America tank top and my oversized cozy grandpa sweater, and minding my own business while watching Captain Marvel, but now I'm at some hick bar without my Cool Ranch Doritos but in the same sexy attire. If my dear, loving sister wasn't right about the fact that I haven't gone out since I caught Shithead cheating on me, I would have resisted more. She normally has better taste than this, though. When we drive from our little country town for an hour, we are normally going toward the city, but not tonight. Tonight, she went to an even smaller, even shittier, even more country town than our home, sweet home. As we enter, her friends call her over, and I don't even bother going with. We do the same song and dance every time we go out. She goes and does the classic white-girl scream when she sees her friends, like it has been years since she last saw them when it has been only about three hours. Tonight, by the looks of it, is one of her friend's birthdays. The pink tiara and matching sash that says "Happy 30th Birthday" gave me the hint.

I find an empty barstool at the end of the bar and plop down. The bar is busier than I thought it would be for a Friday night in a town of five hundred, so I just sit back, in no hurry to grab the bartender's attention. I look around the small place and see a couple of slot machines, a couple of tall tables with large groups of people huddled around them, a jukebox with colored lights racing around the edges, and countless antlers hanging from the ceiling. I bet this classy joint gives you a free drink when you bring in a set of antlers. The buzz of the chitchat is loud, but I can hear Tom Petty's "Free Fallin'" start up and bob my head along. As he starts singing about how he's a bad boy for breaking her heart, I get shoved. I look over to see my caring sister leaning in as she says, "You're doing it again." My habit of humming along to whatever song is on the radio annoys her, but I guess I have some super hearing because no one can ever hear me. I've always done it. I'm guessing it helps with my crippling social anxiety. Any place with more than two people I don't know makes my heart race and my palms sweat. She claims the humming makes me seem stupid and unapproachable, but tonight I think my disheveled look would be more of a turn-off for these deer hunters than my humming along to Tom Petty. But what do I know about love? I mumble my apologies, and she flags over the bartender. She orders some fruity drink that's bound to give her a hangover tomorrow and asks what I want. I just ask the short, fat bartender for a soda. My delightful sister tells her to put a lemon on it so people will think it's a Tito and soda. You know, it is very important that these hicks know what I'm not a square and can drink alcohol. The bartender gives my sister her drink and places my soda with lemon in front of me. My sister leans in and whispers, "Try not to look so awkward." Before I can clap back with a remark, she's gone back to her friends.

I squeeze the lemon into my soda and stir it around with the straw. I hear Jake Owen on the speakers; I don't know what song it is, but I can recognize his voice. I'm not a huge country fan, but I know a lot about it since every small town has a country station. Just then, a tall, heavy man with a bushy beard and a Deadpool shirt sits down next to me and nods in my direction. I just assume that's a "hello"? I'm not sure why, but I'm the total opposite of most women in bars. Normally when approached at a bar, women get all stupid, giggly, and flirty. For whatever reason I just become even more awkward, annoyed, and mean—not on purpose. It just happens. Before I even think, my mouth starts: "So what's it going to be—sullen silence or a mean comment?" It's a quote from *Deadpool*. I'm still staring straight ahead; I could have been talking to anyone. Shit, I could have been talking to myself.

But he turns toward me and sticks his hand out. "Wow, I'm Mitchell, and I believe just fell in love," he says. "The first *Deadpool* is better than the second one."

Well, shit, I think, *he got me*. I turn my gaze to meet his. He's a lot taller than I thought he was, probably a foot taller than my five-feet, four-inches build. He has dreamy brown eyes, but that's about the only attractive quality. His beard is bushy and untamed, his smile is yellow, and his front tooth is chipped. His hair is just as messy as mine, and he looks like he can down two bags of Cool Ranch Doritos and still have room for dinner.

"Yeah, wow," I counter. "You know Ted Bundy met Liz Kloepfer in a bar, right?"

He raises one eyebrow. "He didn't kill Liz, though," he replies.

Well, shit, he got me again. I don't have anything to say. I decide to just ignore him, and he finally stops staring at me. I pull out my phone and open *Wolverine: Enemy of the State*. I don't even notice when I start nodding to Stevie Wonder's *Superstition* playing in the background.

"Are you a bigger fan of music or reading?" Mitchell asks, trying to start up another conversation.

"Maybe if I ignore it, it'll go away."

"Are you always this sweet?" he asks.

I stop reading and look at him. I thought I had said that in my head, but now, looking at him with his head cocked to the side like a sad puppy dog, I actually do feel a little bad. That is the first emotion other than anger and rage I've felt since I caught Shithead cheating on me. I decide to throw the poor guy a bone. I overdramatically put down my phone, take a long sip of my drink, and then let out a huge sigh like I'm going to bare my soul to him.

"So, what exactly is your goal here?" I begin. "Only two reasons a man would approach a lady looking like this: A) You can tell I've been through a rough breakup and you thought you would try your hand at a rebound hookup one-night stand, or B) the nerdy, I-haven't-showered-in-a-week bitchy type is your type?" Again, without noticing I'm doing it, I start nodding along with the Backstreet Boys to "As Long as You Love Me."

"I think I can answer my own question," Mitchell continues. "You like music better. Well, then, I have a bet for you."

For the first time, I notice that he doesn't have a drink—no fake alcohol, no water, no soda, nothing.

Pretty unusual. I raise my eyebrows to indicate he should go on, and he does.

"I'll play three songs on the jukebox, and if you can guess what they are before the singing starts, I'll leave you alone. Forever. If you can't, you let me take you out on a date. A real date, not this little bar."

Who is this guy? I wondered. *Is he part of five-hundred population of this hick town?* I look past him and see my sister and her friends laughing and joking, so I know I'm going to be here for a while. I bring him back into focus, extend my hand, and say, "Deal."

He asks me if I need a refill on my drink before we head over to the jukebox, but I chug down the rest and slam the glass a little harder than I mean too. He looks at me sideways since he believes it's alcohol. We both stand up and make our way over to the jukebox. He stands in front of it, and I lean against it off to the side. I don't need to cheat; I already know I have this in the bag.

He looks at me with a cheesy smile and asks if I am ready.

I roll my eyes, and he understands that's a yes.

Suddenly, I hear it and think, *Damn, this is going to be easy.* I don't move; I just coolly say, "Don't Stop Believing, Journey. Next."

He starts screaming, "Just a small-town girl living in a lonely *woooorld*!"

I swear the whole bar stops and looks at us. I feel my face get bright red. I turn my back to the crowd, and he keeps singing. He finishes the chorus and then takes a bow, telling his adoring fans that the show's over. Some laugh, some clap, and some sing along. I can't figure out if he is a foreigner or a regular.

He makes eye contact with me, and I nod in agreement. He studies the machine and then punches in a code.

I hear the twangy intro to "Heads Carolina, Tails California" by Jo Dee Messina. "You're making these way too easy," I tease. "Maybe you don't want a date with me."

He doesn't even acknowledge what I said as he gets down on his knees so that he's almost eye level with me and starts singing, "Baby, what you say we just get lost?"

I tell him no.

"Leave this one-horse town like two rebels without a cause," he continues.

I tell him no again, but he just keeps going. At least no one is paying attention this time.

"I got people in Boston," he sings. "Ain't your daddy still in Des Moines?"

"No, nope," I reply. "Daddy was never in Des Moines."

I take his hands and try to get him to his feet before the chorus hits and everyone starts staring at us again. Just as I think I've won, he keeps going: "We can pack up tomorrow. Tonight let's flip a coin." He reaches into his pocket to get a coin.

I move over to the jukebox and push "Stop." He freezes like I hit the stop button on *him*. He turns toward me, looking like I just shot an arrow through his heart. I feel bad for a spilt second, but then he's back to his goofy self. He walks back over to the jukebox and tells me to go back to the corner for the last one.

He starts flipping through, and I can't tell if he has a song in mind that he can't find or if he's choosing wisely. He stops, traces along the glass to get the numbers, and puts them in, and then it happens.

I hear it, and all of a sudden, I'm back in Shithead's bed, watching a video on his phone of a little girl drawing a chalk box on a wall. Shithead's favorite band is Tool. I know every Tool song, but I had never seen the music video for "Forty Six & 2." He was in shock that I had never seen it and made me watch it that second. I kept staring at him instead of the phone, and he got annoyed. We didn't even make it to the chorus before he dropped his phone and started tickling me, which led to the first time he kissed me. I hadn't let myself think about that night until just now.

Then Maynard's voice pulls me back to the present, and I see Mitchell's face in shock.

"You lose!" he yells. "I win! You owe me a date!"

I've watched friends become lovers
       Then
Wonder why it can't happen to us

We have a deal:
He never stops treating me like this
I never leave

I'm glad you're happy but I still wish it was me in your arms

*S*he is a handful
He could handle her fire
everlasting love

I knew this day was going to come. Well, I guess I hoped it would come, and I mean that in the nicest way possible. I got her phone call. She was crying so hard that I could barely make out what she was saying. But between the sniffles and sobs, I was able to understand. Now I'm on my way over to her apartment with my armor of wine and ice cream so that we will have snacks while watching hours upon hours of romantic comedies. Because after all, that's what best friends do for each other when the boy we thought was "the one" breaks our hearts into a million pieces.

I hit the Taco Bell drive-thru, and there is a car in front of me. It's one of those situations when I'm in a hurry but I'm not. I want to get there as fast as I humanly can, but I am also nervous to see what I'm about to walk into. I'm thinking of the worst-case scenario—that I have to wrestle her to the ground and rip a knife out of her hands—but she's not that kind of girl. She is probably planning revenge instead—nothing too crazy. Just something Carrie Underwood would do to an ex after finding out he cheated on her. This leads me to my next thought. She never mentioned why he broke up with her. She just called in tears saying that he broke up with her and that she wanted me to come over. I mean, since it was 11:40 at night, what else did I really have to do on a Wednesday night?

As the car ahead of me pulls up, I follow suit, snapping me out of my daze. *What if this is as bad as her last breakup?* I wonder. *The one that took her almost two years to get through?* She cut off all her hair, lost twenty-five pounds, and got a nose ring. It doesn't sound horrible now, but she made me go to the gym with her three times a week at five in the morning, and somehow I managed to lose only ten pounds. But that's beside the point. She wanted to do some crazy *Eat, Pray, Love* shit but didn't want to do it alone and got mad at me when I couldn't quit my job and go travel the world with her. She works remotely, so I told her she should go, but she never did. Then she decided to pick up a new hobby, the drums. The thing about her is that, when she does something, she goes big. Like when she cut her hair, she cut sixteen inches off and got a curly mohawk. There is nothing small about this girl's dreams. She didn't just buy a rubber pad and a pair of drumsticks; she bought the whole drum set.

Turns out she has no rhythm, and her neighbors weren't impressed with it either. So she decided to try her hand at pottery. She found a pottery class and started to make bowls, mugs, and vases. They were nice, but how many pottery dishes does one need? So after that she decided karate would help her lose weight and maybe meet a nice, disciplined man. She was right—that is where she met this asshole.

The car ahead of me drives away, and I place my order. I decide to get a couple extra tacos for breakfast tomorrow and maybe lunch since there is no way I'm going to work tomorrow.

I thought he was an asshole the first time I met him, but I could tell he made her happy so I didn't say anything. After a while, he grew on me. I learned that his humor was just different than mine and he wasn't a bad guy. He treated her all right, at least until this moment. I start to wonder why he broke up with her. He wasn't overly emotional, but I know he cared for her. They *were* very different, though. She loved dancing, singing, pottery, and the city, while he loved hunting, beer, fishing, and the country. They were both new to karate and bonded instantly over that, but that was the only thing they had in common.

I pull away from the speaker and drive up to the window to pay and get my food. I don't think he cheated on her, but he did have a lot of friends who were girls. He was always texting someone whom he would claim was an old friend of the family or someone he went to high school with. but it never seemed to go further than that. He wasn't a good liar, so I don't think that he could keep it a secret if he was sneaking out behind her back. I guess that was a plus on his side. But he was also very honest— some might say *too* honest. Instead of not saying anything, he would say something that would hurt her feelings. Like if she asked, "Do these jeans look okay?" instead of simply saying no, he would say, "No, those jeans make your thighs look massive." She was very insecure about her "thunder thighs," but whether he knew that or not is another story. He didn't say it to be mean; he just said it because that was what he was thinking.

I drive up to the window, and the lady hands me my food. I grab it, put it in my passenger seat, and drive away. Her house is only five minutes from the Taco Bell. I pull out of the parking lot and take a left to get to the stop light.

I just don't understand. They had gotten back from a trip to Florida two weeks ago, where they had an amazing time. They also had just booked their yearly trip to Vegas not even a week ago. So this was not premeditated. It just doesn't add up to me.

I turn at the light and head straight for a couple of

miles, and then I turn left into her apartment complex. I park the car in my usual spot, turn off the car, unbuckle my seat belt, and turn to grab the food. I get out of the car, and soon I see that she's waiting in the apartment lobby for me with her cat, Nugget. She is wearing a big, baggy nightshirt that was probably his. Her short hair is all messy, her eyes are red and swollen from tears, her nose is raw, and her hands are shaking. She's a mess. This is going to be a long night.

*I*f it is not love
Then I don't want it

*D*oes my mental illness make it hard for me to love people, or does it make it hard for people to love me?

*S*ometimes hearts break
Vows don't last
People lie
It's sad but it is how it goes
Sometimes love is not enough
The one we so badly wanted to be "the one" turns into a stranger
Sometimes we fight our demons, but they still win

You made me out to be the villain of this story when all I did was try to show you love the best way I knew. I will be the first to admit that I made mistakes along the way and I wasn't perfect. But if we're being honest, who is? My intentions were always pure and never to hurt you. I always did and still want the best for you. While I'm taking the high road, keeping it classy, and being respectful, you are not playing nice. You are doing things to hurt me, telling lies, making yourself look like some kind of hero. News flash—I never asked you to save me. I was never a damsel and was never in distress. You came in, riding your big black Chevy and thinking I needed to be saved. But you were wrong. There was nothing here to save. I wanted a friend, a partner, and an equal. So now when you tell the story of us, you tell it wrong. You tell everyone you were the hero and I was the villain.

I truly don't know what number online date this is. My friend and I have been on an online dating app for about three months. Every date seems to be worse than the last—macho meatheads who can't hold a conversation, mama's boys who have to call their mothers in the middle of the date, or worse, guys who stand you up. We live in one of the biggest cities in the country, to give you an idea of how many of these dates I have gone on. Tonight, I'm trying something new, or should I say some*one* new. This guy is not my type. My usual type is athletic, is at least six feet, one inch tall (yes, the one inch is very important), has good style (Polos and Doc Martens), has blond hair and blue eyes, has a nice smile, went to college, loves his family (but does not have a weird attachment to his mother), is an involved uncle, and makes six figures as a doctor, dentist, or lawyer. As you can see, I have a very specific type.

My friend convinced me to try someone out of my

comfort zone. Since I wasn't having luck with my normal type, I decided to give it a try. I normally go for drinks so that, if it's a bad date, I can make my getaway quickly but remain polite. This date wanted to go for dinner, and since I was trying something new, I thought, *Sure. Why not?*

He is an electrician, so he went to trade school, which is still college so that box is checked. He is in a bowling league. I guess bowling could be considered athletic. Maybe that box can be checked? He has dark brown hair and green eyes, and he is five feet, ten inches if he stands up straight. He does have a niece whom he watches every Friday when his sister, who is a single mom, works. She's a nurse. They seem close but nothing out of the ordinary. No red flags yet.

I head to a cozy little bar off Ontario Street, step inside, and look around. I recognize him from his dating profile picture instantly. He is wearing a black V-neck and nicely fitted jeans. He's a little heavier than I thought, so maybe bowling is not as athletic of a sport that I once thought it was. But I'm keeping an open mind. He looks like he put some effort into his appearance. His hair is freshly cut, and I can tell he shaved this morning. He has a five-o'clock shadow now, which is cute.

I'm not too fancy. I have a nice, light blue tunic on and a pair of leggings with knee-high boots. I have my long blond hair twisted into a top knot, and I'm not wearing too much makeup. It is a rule I have—don't wear too much makeup on the first date. I don't want to scare them away when they see me without any makeup on. Being in your late thirties is not as easy as being in your twenties, when makeup is more for fun than for a purpose.

He spots me and waves me over to his high-top bar table, on which two IPAs sit. I think, *Great, he ordered a beer for me.* As I reach the table, he doesn't even bother to stand. He says, "Hi, beautiful." I throw up in my mouth a little, but I remind myself to keep an open mind as I lean in for a hug and introduce myself. He pats my back like I'm one of the boys. This isn't going well, right? I sit down on the barstool next to him and wonder why he picked a table with six chairs when there were plenty of two-chaired tables open.

The waitress walks by, and he hands her both beer bottles and asks for another round, and then he asks if I wanted anything. I smile and ask for a gin and tonic. This is going to be a long night. I abandon my mantra about keeping an open mind. I check my watch to see how late I was, since he was already two beers in that I know of. I was only five minutes late. I ask him how long he was waiting for me, and he assures me it wasn't that long. The waitress comes back with his beer and my drink. She hands us each a menu, and I fill with regret.

Why did think I should try something new? I should have kept with my usual dating plan—my type and drinks only. I think for a second. My new plan of attack is to not keep an open mind but to just have fun. I decide, *It's the weekend. I'm never going to see this guy again, so I should just have some fun.* I sip my drink and can feel my whole intention shift. We talk about his niece and my nephew since they are about the same age. We talk about our families and jobs. When the waitress comes back to take our order, he slams the menus down and says, "Two double bacon cheeseburgers, loaded French fries, and two more beers. He looks at me and says, "Is that okay, or do you want onion rings?" I'm in awe. Of all the dates I have been on, not a single man has ordered for me. But I'm here to have fun—he clearly is not my future husband. I can't remember the last time I had a burger, so I nod in agreement. I now know that the nonathleticism of bowling was not what gave him the round stomach; it was definitely the beer. We talk a little more about the neighborhoods we live in and make small talk.

Suddenly, three men walk up to our table and start talking to him. They greet each other with handshakes, introduce themselves to me, and sit down. Is this a date, or did he invite me to guys' night? As soon as the waitress comes back to get the newcomers' drink orders, another one of the boys shows up. Now, this one I don't mind joining us. He's tall; he has sandy blond hair, a beautiful smile, and bright blue eyes; and he is wearing a royal blue Polo. He apologizes for being late and explains that he got caught up at the office. *Could it be a doctor's office or a lawyer's office?* I wonder. The only barstool left open is next to me. He introduces himself to me and asks if he can sit there. My "date"—I use the term loosely—butts in to say that he can sit next to me but shouldn't try anything because I'm with him. I turn my back to him and tell this beautiful stranger that my "date" and I are just friends. Why else would he bring a girl on a date to guys' night? The beautiful stranger laughs.

The waitress brings the cheeseburgers, loaded French fries, beers, and menus for the rest of the guys. My eyes widen when I see how large this burger that was ordered for me is. Since my new mantra is to just have fun, I dig in! Not that I've been on a diet, but I have been watching what I eat and trying to eat better. I enjoy my first cheeseburger in I'm not even sure how long. The bacon is cooked perfectly, the cheese is melted, and the lettuce is crispy. I remove the top bun and squeeze tons of ketchup all over the burger. Then I move on to the loaded French fries. They are salty but not too salty, full of that crispy bacon and melted cheese, and dripping in sour cream. I will need to do extra yoga tomorrow to make up the calories for this meal, but I'm enjoying every bite of it. I'm not paying attention to anyone or anything but my burger.

I hear a deep, sexy voice say, "Wow! I didn't think a tiny little girl like you would be downing double bacon cheeseburgers. I'm impressed. I thought you would be one of those girls that would just eat a salad."

I look up with ketchup dripping off of my chin and smile sheepishly at the beautiful stranger. He smiles back at me. I think I just found my future husband.

*S*it under this mercury tree with me if you dare
      We can watch the venomous sunset
With the hopes and dreams it takes with it
We can wait for the plutonium moon to raise
Bringing with the crime of the night
I'll be you're Bonnie if you be my John Wayne Gacy
We can run from town to town
Taking trophies from our victims
And die younger than Romeo and Juliet

When the time comes, we'll know exactly what to do. This limbo is a crime against the heart. You're taking me for granted, abusing me and my love, blaming me for your shortcomings. Your failures as a man are not my fault. I'm not going to cry or whine. I'm going to simply let you go. You'll realize what you lost. You'll be jealous when you see me with him and he's treating me right, the way you never could, the way you never attempted to. You'll be sad when you come to your senses and realize she will never love you like I could. She is not loyal; she is just a good lay for the night. When you run to her, she'll be in someone else's bed,. for she knows not what loyalty is. You'll call me up, but it'll be too late. I won't answer. You had me. You mistreated me. You lost me. I thought I was fighting for love, but I was letting you manipulate me. When this is all said and done, I'll forget your name.

*J*oe got a cup of Jane

Give me the cliché and I'll rewrite it into something beautiful

Something you have never seen before

That you are craving without even knowing it

You want different—I can make the masterpiece you desire

But it will cost you an arm; since I'm so sweet you can keep your leg

I hope you understand

I hope you're not furious

It may be all Greek to you and possibly Japanese

I promise it'll be worth it if you can keep up with me

You're a skip, a hop, and a broken leg behind me

If you can keep this 6/8 time with me we can make something magical

When you hide behind the curtain you just hide with the other coward magicians

You can't have your cake and eat it too because that's how
you get fat

But then again it's not over till the fat lady sings

It's your choice.

The red pill or the blue pill.

One will take you down the rabbit hole

The other will take you on a magic carpet ride

If you forgot your parachute I wouldn't suggest either one

The madness is a journey not a destination

Either way the sun will set on this day and tomorrow will
come

Stuck under the chain mail

Living in the mind of the needy

Feeding the hearts of the weak

Being held to the wrong standards

Begging to the hopeful

Caring about itself (but no one else)

Pleading with the demons

Dying from the addiction

I stopped missing him when I started missing you

I get off of work early and have some time before yoga, so I decide to pick up a couple things at the grocery store. I have about an hour and a half to kill. I really am in no rush. I leisurely walk through the produce section, picking up peaches and putting them down— mainly just daydreaming about work and dreading my workout—when I hear a voice, one I haven't heard in a long time, say my name in the form of a question. I turn around slowly, and there is my ex-boyfriend from college. I freeze. I'm shocked. It takes me a second to process everything. I have not seen him in person in years. I yelp his name like a little ankle-biting dog and tell him to give me a hug. The last time I saw him was probably at graduation twelve years ago. I'm friends with him on social media, but he is not very up to date on there. He hugs me and gives me a pat on the back. I take a step back and admire him. He looks exactly the same. He has not aged at all—just added another tattoo to finished off his right sleeve of Japanese art. He is wearing a T-shirt, so I can see only up to slightly above the elbow. But his arms are as toned as ever. He stands about five inches over my tiny frame, and his sandy blond hair is in the same cut and style it was all those years ago.

Now, I should use the term *boyfriend* loosely. We met at freshman orientation and then ended up taking a lot of the same classes. We became friends and study partners very quickly. And by the end of sophomore year, we started dating. It was nothing serious. We were both very focused on our studies and never talked about the future, kids, or marriage. By the end of senior year, we decided to go our separate ways. He wanted to go on to grad school in Minnesota, and I wanted to start my career here in Maine. I knew he had no intention of staying here. He always said that he would move once he graduated. He also knew that I would not go with him. We both realized we were operating with a time limit, but we never talked about it and it was never an issue. After we graduated, he packed up the next month and moved to Minnesota. I stayed here.

But now, he is here in the flesh, looking better than ever. And I notice there is no ring on his left ring finger. He looks just as shocked as I am. I wish that I had stayed in my work clothes instead of changing into my yoga clothes. He starts talking a million miles a minute, asking me about my job and my family and Beefy, my bulldog. I can barely keep up with what he is saying. I keep getting distracted by his blue eyes and his smile. He says my name again, and I snap back to reality. Slightly embarrassed, I start giving his words my full attention. I answer the generic questions—family is good, work is good, and Beefy is, well, Beefy. I start to ask the same questions in return, and he goes into much more detail about how his mom was sick the last couple of years but is doing better and his little brother is no longer little and about to graduate college himself with a degree in chemistry. It's all very impressive, but I can't help but notice that he keeps smiling at me.

Is he feeling what I'm feeling? I wonder. It is like no time has passed. The chemistry is strong, and the conversation is easy. He's cuter than I remember, maybe because he is in dress pants and a polo. I mostly saw him in jeans or sweats with a baseball cap on. We talk and laugh and joke and reminisce about the past as we walk up and down the grocery aisles. Every once in a while, one of us will grab something and put it in our basket.

As we talk, I reach down to grab an apple. Because I'm in awe of his perfect smile, I do not realize he is reaching for the same apple. Our hands brush just for a second, but the electricity he sends through me lasts a lot longer.

I could tell he felt it too. He paused in midsentence and looked at me with a shy half smile.

It feels like no time has passed, but I look down at my watch and see it's been almost an hour. He stops me in my tracks and asks if I would like to go get a drink—my choice, water, alcohol, or coffee. *I wasn't crazy,* I think. *We do have some weird magnetic attraction to one another.* I try to be cool and say, "Sure," which came out with way more excitement than I wanted it to.

He grabs his phone, pulls up a number, and calls it. "Hey, baby," he begins. "You'll never believe who I ran into at the store—my old friend from college I told you about. We are going to go out for a drink. Would you like to join so you could meet her?"

My jaw could have hit the floor. I turned and walked away.

*J*ust tell me one thing, how can you just walk away?

Love Grown Cold

"We need to talk"
I know it's coming
But
I can't stop it
I feel my heart breaking
Our time spent together flashes before my heart
I can almost feel your once warm embrace on my skin
And
I know that it's the end
I know I need to find the words to keep you here
""

But I have nothing
I scramble for the words, searching for the line to keep
you here
But nothing comes out, not even a trace of a try
I feel the tears forming in my eyes
But they can't even manage
to find the courage to fall

I don't want this,

I want to go back to our save haven

Before it became haunted.

In that moment

You turn to walk away

My lips tremble and slightly part

As if I had finally found the words

But absolute silence falls out of my mouth

The Instable Reality of the Bipolar Mind

The mind holds hate of which it cannot rid itself. It torments itself repeatedly. Hidden inside is a torture chamber holding family and friends who scream for forgiveness and cry for revenge all at once. Frustration is stuck in the damaged heart of the bipolar mind. Switching the Greek masks quicker than the tide can rush in or out. Worn out and weak. But never tardy. Two in one, trapped in a body with no face. Sex sounds escape the basement while death cries flee from the attic, with absolute silence filling the middle floor. Happiness comes only with death.

Forgive me, Father, for I have sinned. The tortured mind never rests, just keeps riding highs and lows. It is never gray, only black and white. Two in one, but both a frozen hell. Never as romantic as it is made out to be in movies, this state has become home. Familiar and safe:

one yearns for love, the other awaits a warming death. Scattered lies weave in and out of this reality. Calming the mind for only seconds at a time. I'm breathing the air but not receiving the oxygen.

*H*e is not the kind of guy who is looking for forever

Dating Apps

There are dozens of dating apps out there, some better quality than others and some more expensive than others. At the end of the day, they are all used by people looking for the same thing: human connection. Whether it be just physical for the night or emotional for a lifetime, everyone wants the same thing. It doesn't seem like a hard process. I'll explain a little deeper in case you are a lucky one who has never needed to use one of these apps.

You get a buffet of the gender you are looking for, and then you swipe either left or right, depending on whether you are interested or not. Once you match with someone, you can talk. In theory, it does not sound so bad, correct? *Wrong.* Dead wrong! You start a conversation—some of the apps even help you start it—then you start talking about the same things over and over again. "What is your favorite color?" "Where are you from?" "What is your middle name?" Over and over again, the same questions.

If you're like me, you go in deep right away because you don't have time to waste: "What are your stances on politics and religion?" If they cannot handle it, then they can't handle me.

Now, women get a bunch of matches, which sounds great. The problems with this are getting ghosted and not even getting conversations started. Every once in a while, you'll talk all day to the same guy and then, the next morning, *poof*! He is nowhere to be found. You have to make sure you don't get attached too easily. I hear it is even worse for guys. You have to be so tall, make so much money, have never been married before, or have no kids. It sounds like an absolute nightmare.

I don't care about height. I'm five feet, seven inches. If you're shorter than me and it bothers you, that is a you problem, not a me problem. When it comes to money, I don't care. I have my own. As long as you have a job and can support yourself, I don't need your money. Now, when it comes to being married before, I understand, but now that I'm in my thirties, a lot of the people my age have been married, so that doesn't bother me. The kid thing tends to be a little tricky because I don't want any of my own. I do not want to physically carry a baby in my womb and deliver it. That sounds miserable. But I don't hate kids or anything. I would foster or adopt in a heartbeat. For me, children aren't a dealbreaker as long as there is no baby-mama drama. I do not do drama, and I really can't handle it when kids are involved.

I have bashed online dating enough. It is miserable, but I have also seen the upsides of it all. I even met a great guy online. We dated for two years, and then he decided I was no longer what he wanted, which was fine. My best friend found the love of his life online, as have many others. It takes time, patience, and communication, just like love.

I am not looking for love like a Disney movie
I am looking for love like a nineties rock song

When I said I am yours
I meant forever

The Breakup

I can feel it coming …
  The avoidance
There has to be some way to stop it
Maybe we can talk it out

The avoidance
We haven't spoken for three whole days
Maybe we can talk it out
I'll just sit here in silence

We haven't spoken for three whole days
There has to be some way to stop it
I'll just sit here in silence
I can feel it coming …

You're giving me false hope
All you give me is false hope
Hard to trust you when all you give me is false hope

You chose lies and deception

Instead of love and affection

You wanted fentanyl and Adderall

Instead of me and my all

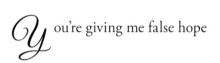 You're giving me false hope

*L*ooks down the barrel
   Bipolar Disorder Two
The safety is off

Run Away

If I ever get close enough to fall in love again
  I think I might just run away
Just pack my bags, not to move into his old farmhouse
But to hit the gravel road
I'll pack an arsenal of things I need to protect my feelings
Guns, a crossbow, and tequila for good measure
I'll steal his old Chevy S10
To get as far away from him as I can
I'll never look back

You don't get to be sad over my broken heart
When you are the one who caused it

Country Boy

Camouflage gives me PTSD
Aaron Rodgers makes me sick
Busch Light makes me throw up
The smell of gasoline burns my nostrils
You get more excited by Kubota than me
Chevy isn't as reliable as you say
There is more to life than sitting in a deer stand
When you said "I love you," I knew I should not have believed you

Reasons I Am Better than Your Girlfriend

- I hate shopping. I'm not into name-brand stuff. Yes, I have clothes from Wal-Mart.
- I have my own job. Therefore, I can pay my own bills. I don't need your money. You keep it.
- I can stand up for myself. When that ugly drunk guy at the bar grabs my ass, I can take care of it. Babe, you just sit and finish your beer.
- My favorite restaurant is Taco Bell. Cheap date.
- I know you have a life outside of me. I'm not clingy. Go watch the Packers beat *da Bears*.
- I don't have a green thumb. You don't have to buy me flowers. I'll just kill them.
- I have a dirtier mind than most men I know. You can't offend me with sexual jokes.
- I've been cheated on, and it is no fun. I'll never do that to you. I'm as loyal as they come.
- I'm just flat-out cuter than she is.

I would have loved you to the end
If you would have let me

Mr. Valentine

Guess it would be safe to say I'm a skeptic. But can you really blame me after it all? The lying? The stealing? The divorce? They say, "Move on. Not everyone is like that." True. I understand, and even worse I agree. But let me explain the best way I can.

Taylor asks, "Is the high worth the pain?" No, it wasn't. Was not at all. Is it ever?

Someone said, "It's better to have loved and lost than to never have loved at all." I'm not sure I'm buying.

The love in these three-minute love songs, two-hour rom-coms, and 421-page Nicholas Sparks books takes a lifetime to create. It takes work. We throw it away the second there is a bump in the road. Why? Why can Grandma and Grandpa make it work but our parents can't?

It's 2022. No one wants to work for it now, when a shiny new toy is at their fingertips.

One sided? Everything about your love was one sided.

PSA: no matter how hard you work, how committed you are, you can't make a relationship work on your own. It is a team sport.

Is sixty years worth it for the day he dies? Judging by the look in her eyes a year later it's not. It's like all the happy memories have been erased. Life's purpose was snuffed out. Any desire to carry on is gone. Is being blue better than being over it? Or was Brendon lying?

Mama raised a girl who doesn't need anyone. The consequence? I don't need anyone. Destiny's Child would be proud of the independent woman I became, but am I?

Does one truly ever fall out of love? I believe not. The good memories will haunt you for an eternity.

I envy her. She's ignorant, not by choice but by nature. She trusts like he never cheated. She thinks it's just a phase. A six-pack a night and a couple shots before work is the norm. The slurring and the shaking are just when he's in a bad mood. It's love, right?

If it even lasts—it doesn't. Not everyone dies like Noah and Allie. Someone still goes on with a broken heart.

Best friend said it best: "You'll risk your life for a cheap rush but won't let anyone in your heart." Maybe she has a good point? Nah, forget that. I'm good. Thanks for the concern, though, friend.

*I*f I fall …
     Will you catch me?
Or will you let me fall?
Will you leave when it get hard?

Will you catch me
When I need you?
Will you leave when it gets hard?
Can we build a life together?

When I need you,
Will you let me fall?
Can we build a life together?
If I fall …

I'm not sure why but, out of all my breakups, this one hurt the worst.

Too Much

It's been a long day at work. Honestly, it has been a long *week* of work, for both of us. We are both tired. We crawl into bed after our nice, warm shower and dinner. We snuggle up in the big, soft blanket he got me for my birthday a couple of weeks ago. I rest my head on his bare chest, and he starts to twist my long, dark curls in his fingers. My hair is still wet from the shower.

He starts to tell me about his day, his coworker's house troubles, the power plant units, and his manager's behavior. It is not that I don't care; it is that I don't understand all the power plant lingo. It has been two years, and you'd think by now I would understand more than I do, but I don't. I continue to listen to him talk, but really, I just love the sound of his voice—the inflections of it when he gets mad and the steadiness of it when he's bored. I glance at the clock behind his head and start to count down the hours until he has to go back to work and I will have to move from my sacred spot on his chest. We rest for a moment. No words. Just silence. It is nice. It is quiet. All I can hear is his heartbeat and his deep breaths.

It is my turn now. He asks about my day. But I don't move except for tracing the letters of his tattoo on his pecs. I tell him all about work—how much I hate it, how I wish we could retire thirty years early, and how I don't want to go tomorrow. He just nods and keeps playing with my hair. He doesn't get annoyed or mad that I'm bitching; he just lets me vent.

He is my calm. He's my peace. He squeezes me tight and tilts my chin up. He gives me a soft, sweet kiss. His lips are soft and smooth as they hit mine. I fall into a dreamlike state, hypnotized by the pattern our bodies have fallen into. We grind together, back and further. We stop, and our eyes lock. He pulls back and asks, "How much do you love me?"

I reply simply, "Probably too much."

I wanted you for the long haul
You wanted me to pass the time

Friends

Have you ever had someone break up with you and then say, "I hope we can still be friends"? If not, you're lucky. If you have, I feel for you. This has happened to me not once but twice now. I have some pretty serious questions about this. Let's start at the beginning: Why would I want to be your friend after you were my best friend, my lover, my world? Now you want to take a demotion and just be my friend? I don't think so. You want to just kick back and not do any of the heavy lifting. You want to just be friends? No, I don't think it works like that. You were the person I thought was "the one," the love of my life, and now you just want to be friends? I'm not sure what that even means. Do you just want to be friendly? Like when I see you in the grocery store, you want me to smile and say hi? Yes, I can do that, not because we are friends but because I'm a mature, adult woman. But if you're thinking I'm now a friend who can come over, drink a couple of beers, and watch the football game, you're wrong. So totally wrong. If what you mean by *friends* is not deleting you off all my social media accounts and blocking your number, yes, I can do that. If you mean friends who will exchange funny memes and Tik Toks, then no. I don't want to make your day better or brighter. I don't want to talk to you on the regular. I don't want to know how you're doing or how the family is. And no, I don't want to be your friend. For the big kicker, if what you mean by *friends* is "friends with benefits," I say this with all the love in my heart: Go fuck yourself. No, I do not want to be your friend.

*N*ow please rest in peace
I loved you, but you hurt me
You are dead to me

*S*he's a rare kind of beauty, one that she doesn't even know that she is. She has long, curly hair and big brown doe eyes. She loves to sing, but dancing is her favorite. She enjoys reading, but writing is where her true passion lies. She loves all animals, but she can't live without dogs. She's a Midwestern girl down to *ope*s and *da*s. She has a big heart that has been through the wringer a couple of times. She is smart in an unconventional way. She has duality: she can be the life of the party or the silent observer. She's an outgoing introvert. She's not afraid of anything. She'll try anything once. She has a work ethic that is hard to beat and is a friend to the environment. She loves nature walks, especially in the fall. She hates to cook but loves to eat, and she has a lot of energy but can fall asleep in minutes. She's been hurt. Her heart is scarred, but she's not scared of the next chapter.

Words on a Page

Focus on the pen. Never look up—just keep writing. Don't look up for, if you do, you'll see who is watching you. Then you will alter your performance. So keep the hand steady and just keep writing. Let the mind wander but keep the hand steady. The more we try to control the mind, the more we lose control over it. It's just like the heart. Both heart and mind will wander wherever they so choose, and no human or medicine can bring them back. Not even a symbolic ring or a vow observed through speech is a match for a mind and heart on a mission. Together they are unstoppable. Good or bad? Well, that's for you to decide. Do choose wisely, I warn you. For your past will guide your present and haunt your future. They say we should live with no regrets, but who are they and what do they know about this? Every time you go back to that thought of regret, you let it win. Yes, you have the choice, but what do you choose? And better yet, why? You'll drive yourself mad trying to figure it out and give yourself a disorder. You'll become like Sybil, but you have no idea what I mean by that so you'll ignore me till later. You'll lie in your bed alone and wonder if I was right. You'll try your hardest to forget my words or to forget my face, but you won't—you can't. You tell yourself pretty little lies to get through the day. Just keep telling yourself this little white lie; it might be little and pretty but it's a lie nonetheless. Tell it to yourself till you feel better and can rest easily. You then begin to veer off subject and wonder about pretty people and beauty, inner beauty and outer. You question whether the soul really is as beautiful as we think and if beauty is just skin deep. But there are no real answers—ever. Only uncertainty and answers that lead to more questions. But we as humans, especially Americans, play God daily as though it doesn't affect anyone but ourselves. We'll play with the fire until we get burned, until God himself strikes us down. This isn't about religion or politics but about two simple questions with two not-so-simple answers: How do you treat people, and how do you view life? Are you as shallow as they say? In your deepest thoughts, your deepest heart answers truthfully, where only you and God (if you choose to believe in one) can hear the answer. Can you admit it to yourself? Does it matter? Does any of this matter? Or is this just a game? An act? A show? A joke? It's not me calling your bluff; it's not me you're lying to.

It's your truth, and darling, trust me—it means absolutely nothing to me. Believe me or don't; it's your choice. We all know how weak you really are. You take the simplest way out for you and yourself only but are no true man. You do things to better yourself only and nothing more. The one and only time you had the chance to pull the trigger, you choked. You pretend for the sake of your reputation that you're fearless, but even the devil and his demons know you're not. By now I have pissed you off by saying everything you never wanted to admit about yourself. You know by now that you're weaker than you ever wanted to acknowledge. Crumple it up and throw it away. It's only words on a page. Now continue with your day.

*Y*ou dispose of your women like you dispose of your beer bottles.

First Act

It's time you grow up and take off the mask. This is your final curtain call. Your acting career is officially over. For years your adoring fans have watched you move gracefully from stage left to stage right, but these petty skits are no longer entertaining the once affectionate crowd. Your formerly adolescent fan base has grown up and carried on with their lives, but you are still stuck playing an imaginary character. If you knew the truth, I think I would get an Academy Award for the act I've made you all believe for so long.

I understand I'm guilty. We were both hurt. I said things that I didn't mean, and you said things you didn't mean. We held each other up at emotional gunpoint. I pulled the trigger when you choked. I knew you had it locked and loaded, but when I pulled the trigger, the best you could do was stroke it. I should have known that's how it would end because that is how it was our whole friendship. I was the strong one, and you were always the weak one. I would carry you and fight your battles. You were all talk, never had the courage to make your dreams come true—only to sit and feel sorry for yourself. That is where you and I differ. I fight tooth and nail for my dreams while you give up when they aren't handed to you. I wanted what was best for you. I wanted you to be happy, but most important, I wanted to you to be safe. I did not want to have to worry. When we fought, you cried and I kept calm, so you didn't believe that I was hurt. I had used up all my empathy on you in the beginning, but now that I am alone, the tears you wanted drench the paper.

$\mathcal{Y}$ou can tell me I'm wrong, but your actions prove that I'm right

They say the past is the past, but what happens when the past does not stay in the past and actually becomes the present so the future is destroyed before we can get out of the present?

The Not-So-Funny Joker

Be careful with your words because they are not a joke to her. When she is the punchline, she is not laughing. What you think is funny can actually scar her for a lifetime. *Sorry* is not an eraser. When metal crashes down on bone, the bone can repair itself within weeks. But when words hit the heart, it cannot mend itself as easily due to the overactive and obsessive mind. It takes longer for the heart to heal than for a broken bone, and unlike that broken bone, the heart doesn't repair itself and come back stronger. Once the heart is broken, it will never be as strong as it once was. Your words can be more deadly than a sword and leave wounds that will never fully heal, even if they were just a joke. Once someone has been told something enough, they will start to believe it, even if it is a lie. And just remember, the words that you say behind her back will eventually get in front of her face.

*H*e's like a puzzle, but I don't know if I have all the pieces. I'm not 100 percent sure what the design is. I do believe it shifts and changes from time to time. I don't know if these pieces are even from the same puzzle. Some are large and fit together easily. I think I can start to tell what the design is. Some are smooth on all the edges and don't connect to anything. There are pieces that are so teeny-tiny that I'm not sure I really need them at all. But the deeper into the puzzle I go, the more I realize that I need all the pieces. Each piece plays an important part in seeing the bigger picture. I only have the pieces he has given me, and I think he's holding onto some. I'm not sure how to get the rest, but I'm patient enough to wait. I'm not great at puzzles, but I do like a challenge and I am a committed person.

If you can't trust your heart or your gut, then ask your guy friend. No, not the one who secretly wants in your pants while you ignore that fact, the one who is like your brother.

If you're not 110 percent sure about a guy, leave him. There are millions more out there.

I'm not sure I got all my clothes in the closet in the first place, but it's like a cartoon the way everything is bursting out of it—shoes, scarves, handbags, dresses, old pictures, sweaters, jewelry, pants, skirts, bras, lotions, and the list goes on and on. Either this closest is the smallest closet I have ever seen or I just have way too much stuff. I'm going to go with the first rather than the latter. I'm a girl, so I can't possibly have too much stuff.

My floor is covered in clothes that I thought were going to look cute, but now I can barely see the beige carpet. The bed is also covered in clothes. I have two stacks: a maybe pile and an I-need-to-still-try-on pile. Each pile is stacked about four outfits high. I thought my French bulldog, Noodle, was on the bed. Either he is asleep under one of the piles or he ran for shelter to the couch in the living room. I don't blame him; I wish I could hide too. I haven't been on a date in about three years, not since I found out that my boyfriend of two years was cheating on me for at least half of that time. I have had no interest in going on a date since. I have been out and flirted here and gotten a phone number there, but nothing has caught my eye.

Then a friend I have known forever asked me out on this date. We are such good friends that I thought he was joking at first. He asked me to go to an art gallery. He's not into art at all, but it's his friend's show and he wants to support him. I thought he was asking me as a friend because he had had a little too much to drink, and it came out as more of a statement than a question. I was also a little tipsy and a little in shock, so I said, "Sure. Why not?" I did not think much about it. To be honest, I totally forgot because the night went on and we continued our game of darts. It wasn't until the next day that he texted me to confirm what time he would be picking me up, and now here we are.

I didn't think I would be this nervous. I'm not sure if it's because I haven't been on an official date in three years or if it's because it's *him*. Maybe a combination?

My hands are sweating as I pull up zipper to this navy-blue cocktail dress. Ugh! No! No! This doesn't look good either. I'm beginning to run out of clothes and time. The dress I wanted to wear looked like a grandma's nightgown, not flattering at all. I mess with the zipper, shimmy out of this dress, and throw it on the no pile. How do I have only three contenders left? I don't have time to look through my mess of a closet to find something else, so I pick the next dress up out of the maybe pile. I slip on the a floor-length, dark purple halter dress. This would be cute if I were going to the beach. I slide the dress down over my hips and take a deep breath. *Is it too late to cancel?* I think. *I can call and say I think I have the 'rona or that Noodle ran away and I had to go find him. No, I can't. He's the kind of guy who would bring me soup or help me find the supposedly lost dog.* I look at the mess of outfits on my bed. They all look hideous, outdated and ugly.

He'll be here in thirty minutes, and I still need to finish my hair and makeup. I try not to think about it. I whip open my closet again and pull out a little red dress from the back. I don't even remember buying it. The tags are still on it. I guess that could explain why I don't remember having it. I shake and shimmy into the knee-length, long-sleeved, lacy, open-back, candy-apple-red dress. Eh! It looks better than anything else I have tried on, so I guess it'll do.

Now shoes. *Ugh! Why do I do this to myself?* He's a good eight inches taller than me, so I am safe to wear heels. I try on my black six-inch Jimmy Choos but look like a hooker, so I go with my low nude heel.

This will work. It *has* to work. I don't have any options left.

I run over to the vanity on the opposite side of my room and crash into the chair to do my hair and makeup. I pull my dark brown curls into a low bun at the nape of my neck. I actually think it looks nice with this dress. This might be coming together after all. I just might be able to pull this off. I stick a couple of bobby pins in the bun to secure it then move my head from side to side to give it the onceover in the mirror. *Not too bad*. Now for makeup. I wanted to do a sexy smoky eye, but time is not on my side tonight so I will settle for bold winged liner with natural eye shadow and a sultry red lip instead. It is now me against the clock. I start my foundation and concealer and rush through it. I put some pink blush on the apples of my cheeks, followed by highlighter on my cheekbones and down the center of my nose. *So far, so good*. Not looking like a model but also not like a troll that lives under a bridge, so I'm going to take that one as a win.

I start on my eyes. I take a neutral beige matte color and swipe it generously over my eyelids. Then I start the outline of the wing on my left eye. The makeup gods must me on my side tonight because it looks perfect, maybe the best winged eyeliner I have ever done. Dare I say it's the best winged eyeliner that has ever winged? Okay, now I'm just getting cocky. I take a second look in the mirror and am pleased with what I see. I am starting to feel confident. I move to the right eye, put the eyeshadow on, and *dammit!* I look like a troll under a bridge. Why do we have to have two eyes? Why is it I can do one eye perfectly while the other eye looks like it was done by a three-year-old with a crayon who doesn't know if he is right-handed or left-handed? I grab a makeup-remover wipe from the drawer of the vanity and forcefully clean off the makeup from my right eye. I start to try again, but my hand is starting to shake.

I take a deep breath, relax my shoulders, and give myself a pep talk: *It's just makeup. It's just eyeliner. It's just a boy. It's just a date. Is it just a date? Is it just a boy? Do I have more feelings for this boy than I want to admit?*

I lace my fingers together and push my arms out in front of me to get a good stretch. I pick up the eyeliner again and breathe out overdramatically. I run the liquid eyeliner pen over my eyelid. Well, it's not as good as my left eye, but I don't look like a troll under a bridge anymore or like the three-year-old with the crayon did it, so it'll do—especially because I am down to ten minutes. I'm starting to get extra nervous that he is going to come early. I'm not done with my makeup. I open the vanity drawer and rummage through my messy makeup drawer to find my favorite mascara. I do two thick coats on each eye. I lean back and admire my work of art for half a second before moving on to my lips. I have my red lipliner and favorite lipstick already sitting out on my vanity. A red lip is kind of my thing. I can do this part in my sleep. I line my lips flawlessly and then fill them in with my lipstick. I smack my lips together. I look at myself in the mirror and give a very weak smile. This is really happening. I look okay, not like a model walking the runway in Milan but definitely good enough to go on a date with a friend to an art gallery.

All I need now are some finishing touches. I make it through the horror scene that is my room to my jewelry box. I unbury a small silver box from the top of my dresser and open the lid. I pull out a small emerald-cut diamond ring that was my mother's engagement ring, a set of matching earrings, and a tennis bracelet. I think for a second as I grab the earrings that I hear the doorbell. I freeze in place.

This is JL Hansen's third
book. Although the style
of this book is different
the passion for poetry and
storytelling is the same.

Printed in the United States
by Baker & Taylor Publisher Services